The Burning Sea

Paul Collins is the author of 140 books, including fantasy series *The Jelindel Chronicles*, *The Quentaris Chronicles* and *The World of Grrym* (in collaboration with Danny Willis).

Sean McMullen is the author of over a hundred fantasy and science fiction novels and stories, including *Souls in the Great Machine* and *Voyage of the Shadowmoon*. He was runner up for the Hugo Award in 2011.

Also by Paul Collins

The Jelindel Chronicles
The Quentaris Chronicles
The World of Grrym (with Danny Willis)
The Earthborn Wars
The Maximus Black Files

Also by Sean McMullen

Before the Storm
Changing Yesterday
The Ancient Hero
Souls in the Great Machine
Glass Dragons
Voyage of the Shadowmoon

THE BURNING SEA

Paul Collins and Sean McMullen

FORD ST

First published by Ford Street Publishing, an imprint of
Hybrid Publishers, PO Box 52, Ormond VIC 3204
Melbourne Victoria Australia
hybridpublishers.com.au

This publication is copyright. Apart from any use
as permitted under the Copyright Act 1968, no part may be
reproduced by any process without prior written permission
from the publisher. Requests and enquiries concerning
reproduction should be addressed to Ford Street Publishing
Pty Ltd, 162 Hoddle Street, Abbotsford, VIC 3067, Australia.
www.fordstreetpublishing.com

First published 2015

National Library of Australia Cataloguing-in-Publication entry
Creator: Collins, Paul, 1954– author.
Title: The burning sea / Paul Collins, Sean McMullen.

ISBN: 9781925000924 (paperback)

Series: Warlock's child: bk 1.

Target Audience: For primary school age.

Subjects: Fantasy fiction.

Other Creators/Contributors:
McMullen, Sean, 1948– author.

Dewey Number: A823.3

© Paul Collins and Sean McMullen

© Cover design: Grant Gittus

© Cover illustration Marc McBride

Editor: Gemma Dean-Furlong

Printing and quality control in China by Tingleman Pty Ltd

To Robyn Donoghue – champion
for Ford Street

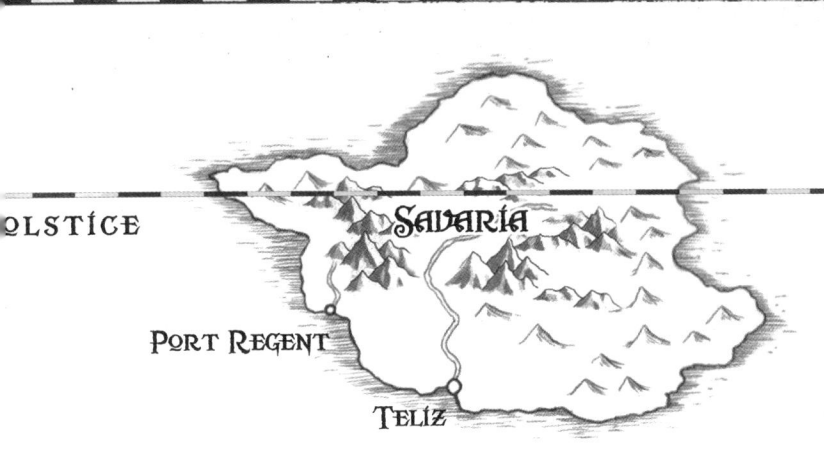

OLSTICE　SAVARIA

PORT REGENT

TELIZ

MORTICAS

CENTRALIAN
SEA

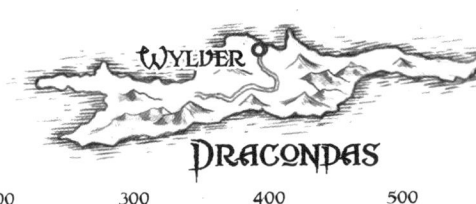
WYLDER

DRACONDAS

| 0 | 100 | 200 | 300 | 400 | 500 |

MILES

DRAGONS

Even an invasion fleet of five hundred ships is not very impressive from three miles above, and the watcher was not impressed. This was because he was bigger and more powerful than any of the warships below.

Dravaud circled lazily on vast wings, reaching out with senses that even the most learned of human wizards could never understand. Something familiar was down there, its presence faint but distinct. It was as tiny as a spark, yet a spark could set an entire city ablaze.

The fleet was following a bank of fog the size of a province, and both were driven along by the same wind. A netting of enchantment, more finely spun than a spider's web, bound the fog at its edges, and the right words of unbinding would dissolve the netting and disperse the fog.

By then it would be too late for the enemy.

The dragon continued to circle, maintaining his height while he decided on which ship to select. There was the hint of another dragon down there. *Only an egg or a hatchling, just a hint of life that is more than life. Are the humans taking a dragon chick into battle? Why would they do that?*

DANTAR

For Dantar, the sight of the distant dragon was both exciting and terrifying. Although dragons seldom took an interest in human affairs, they were enormous and unpredictable, so humans had to take an interest in them. If the dark, winged speck against the blue sky concluded that a few dozen burning warships would look pretty, it would not hesitate to plunge out of the sky and attack.

The weather seemed too good. In the epics that Dantar had read, great battles happened under cloudy skies, with lightning flashing in the background. On this day the sky was clear, the sea calm and the wind steady and predictable. It was as if the dragon had got the date for its attack wrong.

I'm fourteen and I should be at home, playing with the

cat and doing homework, thought Dantar. *Fourteen is a bad age to die. So is fifteen. Why am I here? My family is rich, I don't need to work as a cabin boy on a warship.*

Not a single member of the *Invincible*'s crew was below deck. Even Dantar and the three other cabin boys had been given light crossbows and told to fire at the dragon if it attacked. From the way his hands were shaking, Dantar doubted that he could hit even something the size of a ship.

All along the mid-deck the marines and sailors stood with their bows and crossbows ready, and on the forecastle and quarterdeck the artillery crews were standing by their ballistas and arbalests. If the dragon attacked it would be met with a cloud of iron bolts, arrows, firepots and arbalest lances.

Will it even notice? Dantar wondered.

Dantar was dressed as a very small sailor, and the sailors all wore white tunics over white trousers, so that they could be seen more easily if they fell overboard.

The ship was strangely quiet, and hardly anyone spoke. It was as if everyone aboard was preparing for death, because one puff of the dragon's breath was all that was needed to destroy the ship.

The ship's wizards and shapecasters were on the forecastle, their hands shimmering as they wove and shaped castings. They were a better defence than all the other weapons put together. Air shapers could put turbulent winds under the dragon's wings, and castings by the water shapers were the only shields against the firestorm of a dragon's breath. The shapers wore robes that flowed like silk yet gleamed in the sunlight like polished steel. The cloth was indeed some sort of magical armour.

'What's a good age to die?' Dantar asked aloud.

'Maybe ninety?' said Marko, the older youth standing next to him.

'Sounds fair. I'm fourteen, so why can't I come back in seventy-six years and face certain death?'

'Because you'd be hanged for desertion.'

'But I want to finish growing, meet girls, and get a deep voice. Instead I'm here.'

'I'm here too.'

'Aye, but you're seventeen.'

Marko was everything that Dantar was not. Tall and blond, he was handsome enough to be in the king's personal guard, and he already had a beard. When he smiled his face was strangely lop-sided, though, as if he were too sad to smile with the whole of his face. He was the closest thing to a friend that Dantar had on the ship.

Dantar thought that the best thing about his own body was that it was not much of a target. He was short, wiry and thin, and looked younger than his age. His black hair let him merge into shadows and hide, but if the entire ship got flamed, being good at hiding would not keep him alive.

About half of the people on the *Invincible* were new to the ship, and many of those had never met before they had come aboard. Dantar had been carrying a book when he had boarded the ship at Haldan, and Marko had come up to him and asked if he could borrow it when he had finished. Sailors who could read were rare, and for Dantar the ship seemed full of threatening strangers, so he was very relieved to have Marko as a friend.

'Don't worry, the dragon won't attack,' said

Marko, who could hear Dantar's teeth chattering.

'So it's going away?' asked Dantar.

'Just flying in circles. Dragons like to watch battles.'

'Why?'

'I don't know. Ask a dragon.'

Up on the quarterdeck, someone was shouting. Dantar caught only a few words, mostly about lost surprise, lost advantage, and the cat being out of the bag.

'The admiral's spitting nails because the Savarians will be able to see the dragon circling,' said Marko. 'They'll know it's looking at something behind the enchanted fog.'

'Us?' said Dantar.

'That's it. Something has to be pretty impressive to catch a dragon's attention, and our fleet qualifies as impressive. Oh no! Brace yourself.'

Dantar took that as a cue to look up at the sky. The distant shape had broken off its circling, folded back its wings, and was dropping like a stone.

'The dragon's building up speed before attacking,' said Marko.

'Why attack us? We're not being rude or anything.'

'Dragons always attack the stronger side just before a battle.'

'So dragons like losers?'

'No, no! It's to show that no matter how powerful humans might think they are, dragons are way ahead.'

'We know that already!'

'Nothing to worry about, trust me.'

The dragon spread its wings and leveled out, then came in low, barely above mast height, cutting across the vanguard of the fleet. Dantar watched as the winged shape grew and grew, heading straight for the *Invincible*.

This is it. I wonder if fish like char-roasted human, Dantar thought as wings wider than most villages drove the huge body toward them.

Its mouth opened and fire glowed green deep within its throat. Each tooth was bigger than Dantar was tall, and it had a lot of teeth. Its scales were as bright as polished steel, and enormous eyes saw him yet looked through him. The sharp spines that fringed its face and its head crest were folded back. Dantar had read that dragons did that before attacking.

'Steady! Steady!' shouted the marshal-at-arms. 'Wait for my word . . . Fire at will!'

The dragon's head was squarely in the sighting notch of Dantar's crossbow as he squeezed the release lever. The air in front of him went grey with arrows, crossbow bolts and arbalest lances. Fire pots from the ballistas burst in splashes of flame along the dragon's body, then green flames gushed from between its jaws.

This is going to really hurt, thought Dantar.

The flames poured through the uppermost rigging of the *Invincible*, then the enormous underside of the dragon swept over the ship.

We didn't even scratch it! thought Dantar. Turning, he saw that the warship sailing next to them was smothered in flames, and the dragon was ascending again, driving upwards with ponderous flaps of its huge wings.

'Reload and stand ready!' shouted the marshal-at-arms.

The stricken ship was blazing from forecastle to quarterdeck, and other ships steered to avoid it. Sailors were already climbing the ratlines with douse cloths to combat the fires in the *Invincible*'s rigging.

'All dousers, weapons down and get into the rigging!' shouted the warden of fires. 'All dousers, get up to the fires.'

Dantar and Marko clipped cloths dripping with seawater to their belts and scrambled up into the rigging. Dantar looked back to the inferno that was the *Intrepid* as he climbed.

'Why don't we stop to rescue survivors from the *Intrepid*?' he cried.

'Because everyone aboard is dead!' replied Marko. 'And because –'

A yellow fireball erupted from the *Intrepid*, splashing burning oil hundreds of feet out across the water.

'And because barrels of lamp oil explode if you put them in a fire.'

'I thought *we* were dead,' said Dantar.

'So did I.'

'What? You said we would be all right!'

'I lied. The dragon had us lined up, then it turned its head and flamed the flagship. Dragons never flame flagships.'

'What do I say if some girl asks what I did when the dragon attacked? "Well, I peed my pants".'

'Did you?'

'No, but it was a near thing.'

VELZA

It had not been a good day for Dantar's sister Velza. Normally fire magic was the most spectacular of the four casting types. Air magic was just shimmers, winds and fogs, water magic could raise waves and manipulate water to shape itself into tubes and shields, while earth magic could weaken walls or strengthen weapons. Fire magic castings were literally tangles of green fire, the same as dragons breathed, so that fire shapecasters could fight like very small dragons. Unfortunately, fire magic did not work over water.

The ship's fire shapers were given crossbows, sworn in as marines, and told to shoot at the dragon when so ordered. The twelve shapers were divided into four squads.

Velza coped with being a young woman in an

intensely male society by playing down anything that distinguished her as female. She wore her long brown hair tightly coiled and pinned up, wore the same knee boots and trousers as the male shapecasters, and had a white officer's shirt under her shapecaster's surcoat. She countered the fact that she was pretty by being cold or abrasive to everyone, and exercised on deck more than most of the men.

Now Velza was feeling foolish, because she and her squad could not use their fire shapecasting skills. She tended to blame herself for everything that went wrong, even things out of her control, so she was feeling strangely guilty because the dragon was attacking. As the enormous winged shape bore down on the ship, she ran through a checklist before her mind's eye. This was her first time in action, and although she was frightened, she kept herself steady by trying to distract herself from the danger.

Crossbow loaded, sights adjusted, squad check – Squad check! Do squad check!

'Shapecaster Pandas, check that your string is behind the bolt,' she shouted. 'Shapecaster Latsar, wait for the order to shoot this time!'

'Checking, Captain,' said Pandas.

'Aye, Captain,' said Latsar.

In the distance a cavernous mouth opened; a knight on horseback could have ridden in without touching the sides.

Shooting at that thing will only antagonise it, thought Velza. *Why draw attention to ourselves?*

In spite of her doubts, Velza fired on command and saw her bolt streak into the dragon's mouth and vaporise with a bright flash. The dragon swooped over the ship, ignoring the barrage that rose to meet it. Someone nearby was screaming with agony. Velza looked around.

Pandas had shot himself and was writhing about in a circle centred on the crossbow bolt that pinned his foot to the deck. Velza and Latsar held him down while a carpenter's apprentice was fetched.

'At least you can tell the girls you were wounded in action,' Latsar joked as the apprentice drew the bolt out with a lever clamp.

Pandas continued to scream.

'You're letting the squad down, Pandas!' Velza hissed. 'The whole ship can hear. Bear the pain like a warrior.'

If Pandas heard her words, they had no effect. The surgeon arrived, and he was one of those annoyingly cheery little men who thought you could help people cope with pain by joking about it. Although he was hardly taller than Dantar, he had a very strong presence among the crew, perhaps because he so often stood between an injured man and death. Velza guessed that he was one of the oldest aboard the ship from his short grey hair and beard, yet he was fitter and more energetic than even her.

'I'm afraid there's no hope for your boot,' he said as he sliced the expensive boot off the youth's injured foot. 'Now this will make you feel better.'

He poured sharply scented oil on the wound. This made Pandas scream even louder.

'No bones damaged, you're very lucky,' the surgeon said as he bound up the wound.

Pandas continued to scream.

'You're also lucky nobody else was injured, it's such a slight wound that I'd not bother with it after a real battle. On your way, now.'

Velza and Latsar carried Pandas off to the infirmary cabins under the forecastle.

Velza was both a female shapecaster and

an officer. While there were other female shapecasters in the fleet, Velza had a problem not shared by the others: her father was the fleet's battle warlock, outranked only by the admiral himself. Nobody actually said that her rank had been gained by her father's influence, but a single mistake was sure to get tongues whispering, so Velza never made mistakes. Now one of her squad had shot at himself instead of the dragon, which was practically impossible to do by accident. There would be trouble.

'Why did he have to scream so much?' she muttered as she and Latsar stood staring at the distant patch of burning oil that had once been the *Intrepid*.

'It might have been the crossbow bolt through his foot,' Latsar replied.

'The whole ship heard.'

'And some of the other ships nearby, quite probably.'

'What will the marshal think?'

'He will probably charge Pandas with cowardice.'

'It was an accident. Pandas is too much of a coward to shoot himself deliberately. I shall have to prove that, Latsar. If I don't, he will be hanged from a yardarm. Why did he have to do it? It will go on my record.'

'Some people just don't think, Captain.'

Although Pandas was the scholar of the squad, Latsar was the cleverest of them. Nobody ever won an argument with Latsar.

What now? Velza wondered wearily. *Follow rules. Rule B17: Interview survivors and write a squad report.*

'I must start my squad report, Latsar,' she said. 'Did you hit the dragon?'

'I hit the soft bit under its wing, but it was not very soft,' said Latsar. 'The bolt bounced off.'

'I hit it right in the mouth, but it didn't notice.'

'Will you interview Pandas?'

'No, I already know what he hit.'

DANTAR

It took an hour to put out the smouldering spots in the rigging of the *Invincible*. All the while, the marines were down on the deck, snuffing fires started by burning tar dripping from the ropes. Dantar and Marko were ordered to stay aloft, to douse any new fires that broke out amid the sails.

'So it's true what the old sailors say about war,' said Dantar, as they sat on a yardarm, looking back over the fleet.

'What's that?' asked Marko.

'That it's months of being bored, followed by a few moments of total terror.'

'Not always. A sea battle against other humans can last for hours.'

'Is that worse than a dragon, Marko?'

'Oh aye. It's all blood, bodies, fires, screams,

swords clanging and arrows whizzing past – except for this one.'

Marko pulled his tunic down to show a scar on his shoulder. Dantar put a hand over his eyes and took a deep breath.

'I was lucky, I fell overboard and drifted away,' Marko continued.

'You call that lucky?'

'Oh aye. Everyone was on deck, fighting enemy boarders. Nobody was left below to douse smokers, and a fire started in the oil store. The ship exploded like the *Intrepid*.'

From below came three toots from a whistle.

'There's the order to climb down,' said Marko. 'The riggers and carpenters can repair the mess up here.'

Dantar looked up at the mainmast. The last ten feet were missing.

'Marko, what happened to the crow's nest?'

'Same thing that happened to the lookout in the crow's nest.'

Dantar had begun the voyage with no useful skills. His father insisted that his two children come with him on the *Invincible*, but the captain insisted that the warship would carry nobody who did not work or fight, so Dantar was made a cabin boy.

The trip had got off to a good start when his sister had been seasick for the first three days, yet Dantar had got his sea legs straight away. He had learned that cabin boys did much more than clean cabins, carry meals to the officers, wash their plates, and fire a crossbow occasionally. Dantar also had to catch rats, stoke the kitchen fires, boil water, wash the officers' clothes, go on watch, scrub the deck, and splice rope.

For a boy brought up in the royal palace as the son of the emperor's battle warlock, it was an exciting new world, rather than hard, tedious work. The other children of nobles would not survive long without servants to look after them and their parents to pay for everything, but Dantar now had a trade and felt as if he could run away from his sheltered life back in the capital, Haldan, and live a new life.

It was also his job to stop the ship catching fire.

Sparks sometimes escaped the cooking hearths, so he had to patrol the galley for smokers, a brass bound pail sloshing by his side.

'You've got the most important job on the ship,' had been what old Gyan, the earth-magic wizard, had said when Dantar came aboard.

'Truly?' Dantar had gasped. 'Then why don't they give it to someone important?'

'The penalty's death for not doing it properly. The *Invincible*'s made of wood and has barrels of lamp oil aboard for the flame-throwers and fire pots. We take smoker patrol very seriously.'

The threat of death did add some glamour to the job, but today it was hard, sweaty work. A huge number of smoking fragments had fallen after the dragon's breath blazed through the upper rigging. Soon Dantar's trouser legs were drenched, and his hands were red-raw from tossing the pail over the side on a rope, then hauling it up full of seawater. Eventually the midshipman determined that the smokers were all doused, and Dantar was sent down to the galley.

Being short and thin, Dantar could get into narrow spaces where stray sparks might smoulder, grow, and flare up into a deadly blaze. Being fast helped Dantar dodge the cook's fists. Cook hated everybody, from the admiral right down to the cabin boys. He was a good cook, but not even he could make salt pork, baked biscuit and flatbread taste any better than pretty bad. Everyone complained about the food, so his temper was worst at mealtimes. He took it out on the closest person to hand – Dantar.

Retaliation was not a good idea. A month earlier, Dantar had switched the salt and the sugar, so that the officers got mugs of salty tea. The cook accused Dantar. Dantar accused the cook. There was no proof that either of them had done it, so the marshal-at-arms sentenced the cook to five lashes and Dantar to a caning.

Dantar had slept on his stomach for a week afterwards, but it earned him a reputation for being tough. He had managed not to cry, although he had screamed a lot.

Cook was in a particularly bad mood after having to do smoker patrol by himself while Dantar was busy in the rigging. Dantar watched as he prepared the tray with the tea for the officers. After a suspicious glance at Dantar, Cook took a pinch of sugar from the jar and tasted it.

'Wipe that grin off your face, daft bilge rat!'

Dantar made his face go blank, and ducked under Cook's backhand. He made for the door while Cook decided whether or not to chase him. Chasing Dantar would have meant being late with the tea, which was a bad idea. The officers were sure to be edgy after the one-sided battle with the dragon.

'Oi there, boy, are ye blind?' Cook shouted, then flipped a burning coal from the hearth. It landed near a barrel of olive oil. 'If that blows, it'll sink the whole bleedin' ship.'

That was true. Olive oil burned well enough to be used in flamethrowers.

'I'll tell the marshal you dropped that coal there,' said Dantar.

'It's your word against mine again. We'd both get hanged.'

If we live long enough to face the marshal's court, thought Dantar, recalling what happened to the *Intrepid*. Thinking quickly, he dipped the douse cloth in his pail, balled it up and threw it. It passed between the cook's legs and hit the glowing coal squarely. Unable to lure Dantar close enough to smack, Cook picked up the tea tray and stamped off.

'Smoker!' someone shouted from the oil store.

Dantar dashed down the passageway and into the storeroom as a sailor hurried out with a load of fire pots on his shoulder. He saw a tendril of smoke where a cluster of speaking tubes came through the wall. This was part of a network of pipes that connected important parts of the ship, allowing the captain to give orders without leaving the quarterdeck.

Someone very stupid had been smoking in the storeroom. The idiot had knocked his pipe out against a leather and beeswax tube, and the embers had burned right through it. Dantar dabbed out the embers with his douse cloth. *A broken speaking tube during a battle could get the ship sunk,* he thought. *I'm on the ship and I can't swim.*

Dantar hurried out to the rigging lockers, and returned with a canvas patch and a pot of tar. He was about to wrap the hole in the tube when he heard muffled voices coming from it. Only senior officers used the speaking tubes, so even hearing an indistinct voice from one made him feel important.

I'm Dantar of the House of Barronfeld, master spy, he thought. *No secret is safe from me.*

He glanced over his shoulder, making sure he was alone, then pressed his ear to the hole.

'. . . sure he can be trusted?'

'. . . not your concern!' snapped a vaguely familiar but muffled voice, one clearly used to command. 'Just be ready . . .'

The conversation continued in tight whispers, but Dantar was not able to make out very much.

'. . . give the traitor his reward . . .' said the commanding voice.

Suddenly it was no longer a fantasy game. There was a real traitor. Who? Which side was the traitor on?

Which side am I meant to be on? Dantar wondered.

Heavy footsteps thudded along the passageway outside. Dantar jerked up, quickly wound the patch onto the tube and slopped some tar on top as Cook stuck his mastiff-shaped head in the doorway.

'Get a move on, boy! You're supposed to be on smoker patrol.'

'A smoker burned through this pipe –'

'Then call the carpenter to fix it! Your job is to

douse the smokers, that's all.'

For the rest of his shift Dantar could think of nothing but the voices in the tube. Who had been speaking? Who was the traitor? Was the traitor trying to sink the ship? How long did it take to learn to swim?

VELZA

Once Pandas had stopped screaming, a court of the marshal-at-arms was convened in the master cabin under the quarterdeck. This was the largest cabin on the ship, and was meant to impress and intimidate anyone entering. There were gilt work carvings around the leadlight windows, and brightly patterned Varlinese rugs on the floor. The curtains of the side windows were drawn, and the officers' dining table had been moved so the light from the stern windows was in the eyes of the accused.

Nine senior officers sat behind this table, all dressed in blue knee coats with gold buttons. Facing them, standing, were Velza, Latsar and Pandas. Pandas had injured himself in battle, and people sometimes did this to avoid the fighting. It was technically desertion, and desertion was punishable by hanging.

Pandas is not yet shaving, and he could stand to lose a few pounds, thought the very worried Velza as they entered the master cabin. *He doesn't look heroic, and not looking heroic is bad when charged with desertion. Must have Latsar teach him to look heroic.*

'Before we begin, I must announce that due to the dragon destroying the flagship, the *Invincible* now leads the fleet,' said the marshal-at-arms. 'Vice Admiral Dalzico is now Admiral Dalzico, and this crew must set a good example for the other ships. If that means hanging a few cowards from the yardarm, I'll do it. Squad Captain Velza, please read your report on the dragon's attack.'

Velza did as ordered, and added that Pandas was very clumsy with weapons.

'Thus I told him to check the bowstring. He held the front of the crossbow between his feet to seat the string properly.'

'How did he manage to shoot himself in the foot when the bolt was pointed at the deck between his feet?' asked the marshal-at-arms.

'When he grasped the stock to raise it, he squeezed the release lever by accident,' said Velza.

'Or on purpose. Do you have anything else to say about Shapecaster Pandas?'

'Pandas is only fifteen, Sir, but he is not a coward. I'd stake my reputation on it.'

'But this was his first time in action, and against a dragon. You may stand aside, Squad Captain Velza. Shapecaster Latsar, step forward.'

'Sir,' said Latsar smartly.

Several senior officers smiled and nodded. Latsar was seventeen, but he looked older and moved with the confident swagger of a warrior. When the ship had sailed, several girls had stood on the dock, throwing flowers, calling his name and crying.

Pandas looks like he should be shelving books in some library, but Latsar could be a handsome young prince, thought Velza. The court will believe whatever Latsar says. He's all muscles, bravado and windswept hair. He inspires confidence . . .

Velza snapped her thoughts back to the court.

'Shapecaster Latsar, did the accused deliberately shoot himself?' asked the marshal-at-arms.

'No, Sir.'

'No? Did you see him do it?'

'No, Sir.'

'Then why do you say he's innocent?'

'Nobody wishing to flee from an approaching dragon would deliberately pin himself to the deck, in the line of fire. It had to be an accident.'

Will they accept that? thought Velza, her face burning with embarrassment. *Will they suspect that I briefed Latsar to say that?*

The marshal raised his eyebrows, then nodded. They were thick, bushy eyebrows, so when he moved them they caught people's attention. He wrote on the paper in front of him, taking his time, to make Pandas squirm, and finally folded his hands on the table.

'Shapecaster Pandas, step forward to hear the verdict of this court.'

Velza and Latsar took Pandas by the arms and stepped him forward. Velza felt him trembling with terror.

'Officers of my court, you have heard the testimonies of the accused and those who witnessed the incident. Those who vote guilty, declare yourselves.'

Four officers held their fists out with their thumbs down.

'Those who vote innocent, declare yourselves.'

The other four officers raised their thumbs.

'It appears that I have the casting vote,' said the marshal. 'I suppose nobody in his right mind would pin himself down if he intended to flee. I, Marshal-at-Arms Florantas d'Civaros, raise my thumb for innocence, but –'

Pandas's legs buckled with relief and he dragged Velza down as he fell. Latsar helped them back up. The marshal-at-arms frowned and drummed his fingers on the table as he waited.

'To continue: it is my opinion that Shapecaster Pandas displayed gross incompetence handling his crossbow, and that cannot be allowed on a warship. Shapecaster Pandas, you will load and discharge an armoury crossbow fifty times before you are permitted to return to your bunk. For every misload you will be given one stroke of the cane on your backside by the sergeant of irregulars.'

Leaning heavily on a wooden crutch, Pandas followed the marshal and the officers of the court out of the cabin and onto the mid-deck. For a moment Velza was left alone with Latsar. Taking him by the arm, she leaned so close that her lips brushed his ear and whispered, 'Well done.'

'Your plan,' he replied with a slow wink.

Did he mean that, or was he just being polite? Velza wondered as they walked out onto the mid-deck. *Do boys like him like strong girls like me or brainless tavern wenches? I suppose I'll never find out, not while I command him.*

They joined Pandas, who was waiting to serve his sentence. The officers were gathered near the mast, chatting among themselves while the armourer and sergeant of irregulars were fetched.

'Can't this be postponed?' muttered Pandas. 'I'm in agony, and my foot is bleeding through the bandages.'

'You escaped death by a single vote,' hissed Velza between clenched teeth. 'Don't complain.'

'We shouldn't be here, anyway. There's no real reason to go to war.'

'The emperor ordered it,' said Latsar. 'Savarian wizards are trying to join the four magics back together.'

'We don't know that,' said Pandas.

'Spies reported it,' said Velza.

'Who are these spies, anyway?' said Pandas.

'Spies have to remain secret,' said Velza.

'So there's no real proof that the Savarians are practising forbidden magics?' asked Pandas.

That question borders on treason, thought Velza, who remained silent.

'Technically, no,' said Latsar after a moment.

'So we're off to war for no good reason, and being led by an incompetent nobleman against an enemy that wiped out the first fleet that the emperor sent,' said Pandas.

'Technically, yes,' replied Latsar.

'Saying that about the admiral can get you hanged!' protested Velza.

'His family owes my family money, I can say what I like about him,' said Pandas, who then added, 'Sir.'

The armourer arrived with a crossbow and a bag of wooden practice bolts, followed by the sergeant of irregulars with a cane. Sergeant Haldigar had the burly build and shaven head of an executioner, yet he also had a definite sense of humour. Before any flogging or caning he removed his white tunic to display his muscles to whoever was to be punished, and made a point of smiling. He never smiled at any other time.

This ensured that his victims were thoroughly terrified even before the first blow fell.

Pandas removed his cloak. Velza and Latsar stood back to watch as he slowly, carefully, loaded the first practice bolt. There was a crisp snap as he shot the bolt over the side of the ship.

'Good work,' said Velza softly. 'You saved him.'

'I just spoke the facts as you wanted them spoken,' replied Latsar.

'Without the words coming from your mouth, he would be dangling from a yardarm by now.'

'Surely not, Sir.'

'Surely so, Latsar. I know how the minds of the marshal and his officers work. They had to hear the crucial words from you. They think that because I am a girl, I would let mercy cloud my judgement.'

'I'm sure a merciful thought has never entered your mind, Sir.'

'Why thank you, Latsar. Do you really mean that?'

'Certainly, Sir.'

Most of the crew is watching, thought Velza. *Should do some training, set a good example.*

'We will practise fire attacks while we wait,' she decided. 'Fetch the practice balls.'

'Sir!' said Latsar, saluting.

DANTAR

When Dantar's shift finally ended in the late afternoon, he was no longer the same cabin boy he had been that morning. He had heard secret, important things. People could be murdered for knowing what they were not meant to know. *Should I tell someone?* he wondered as he made his way to the mid-deck, keeping out of people's way. He was not really sure who the speakers had been. The speakers did not know about him, so that kept him safe.

Dantar finally sat down near Blind Gyan, the earth wizard. He was sitting alone, stroking a sword's blade and chanting in some arcane language. Gyan worked earth-magic strength into the metal of swords, so he was popular. Nobody wanted their blade to snap during a battle.

Gyan's a good man, he's safe to ask for advice, thought Dantar, yet still he hesitated. Nearby, someone was firing a crossbow. After several crisp snaps of the bowstring, Dantar heard the thud of a misload – followed by the smack of a cane on trousers and a yelp of pain.

'Bad day for young Pandas from your sister's squad,' said Gyan.

How does he know it's me? Dantar wondered.

'I heard he shot himself in the foot,' Dantar replied.

'He did that too.'

'Aren't fire shapers too special to be flogged or caned?'

'Nah, lad. While at sea they've got no magic. Anyway, flogging is good for an officer's career.'

'What?' exclaimed Dantar, astounded. 'How so?'

'Sailors and marines respect an officer who knows what they go through. A few scars on an officer's back inspires loyalty.'

'Pandas is getting caned on the bottom.'

'That's a child's punishment, it doesn't count. When he's seventeen, he'll need to get himself flogged properly – on the bare back.'

Dantar glanced to the forecastle. His sister was tossing green practice balls back and forth with Shapecaster Latsar. *He would know what to do if he heard voices plotting treason. I wish I'd never heard the voices.* Had one of them really said 'traitor'? Perhaps he'd said 'trader'? He shook his head irritably. It wasn't his business either way. The speaking tubes were strictly for officers, not cabin boys. If anyone knew he'd been eavesdropping, he'd be caned – on his backside.

Someone set me up, he concluded. Seamen were notorious tricksters, everybody knew that. Then again, perhaps the ship would be sunk if he did *not* tell someone what he had heard. What to do? Overhead, the sails and tarry rigging flapped and creaked in the wind. It all sounded reassuringly normal, apart from the occasional thump of a misload, whack of a cane, and cry of pain from Pandas.

Velza looked authoritative wearing the high, flared collar of an officer. The ship's marshal-at-arms was watching her at practice. *I bet she gets a promotion soon*, thought Dantar. *Hope she doesn't get to command me.*

There was another misload, a whack and a

shriek. Coins were exchanged between laughing sailors, betting on how many strokes Pandas would get.

'Bet you a copper he reaches fifty without another misload,' said Gyan.

'Done,' said Dantar.

Poor sod, Velza must wish it were me getting caned, thought Dantar. He looked across to his sister again. She was looking right at him, and staring at an officer meant a caning, so he turned to Gyan and folded his arms tightly. Dantar's mother had died when he was born, so until Calbaras remarried, Velza had provided the discipline in Dantar's life. Dantar had been nearly twelve before he realised that not all girls shouted at you continually and swatted you with a cane. Now she was an officer, and could order other people to cane him.

'I wish I could do it,' he said.

'Give people a caning?' asked Gyan.

'Magic.'

Gyan reached out a gnarled hand and patted Dantar's arm.

How does he always know where to reach? Dantar

wondered. *He's blind. Or maybe he's not quite blind.*

'Being good at magic isn't everything,' said Gyan.

'You can say that because you *are* good at it,' said Dantar.

Gyan shrugged. Dantar looked at the old man's face. It had so many wrinkles, it might have been a map of all the places he'd been. Had each place left a line on him? Would they both get a line to mark this voyage?

'Fifty!' called the sergeant of irregulars.

There was the jingle of more coins changing hands as wagers were settled. Dantar handed a copper to Gyan, then looked across to Pandas and saw Velza give him back his tunic and cloak. Latsar took Pandas by the arm as he began to limp away, but was shaken off. Pandas immediately tripped and fell. Dantar was tempted to laugh, but he could get caned for laughing at a shapecaster.

Gyan was still moving his hands up and down the blade of the sword, caressing the metal. Earth magic worked over water, but was not as potent.

'Why are there four separate human magics?' Dantar asked. 'Dragons have four magics in one.'

'Aye, and that's why dragons' fire castings work over water,' replied Gyan. 'Which is your favourite magic?'

Wait a moment, Gyan's trying to change the subject! thought Dantar.

'Why does human magic come in four types?' Dantar insisted. 'Why can't our wizards master more than one?'

Gyan pretended to sew his lips shut. 'If I told you, I'd have to cut your throat!' he whispered.

'How would you know where I am?'

With a movement as smooth as water pouring from a jug, Gyan swung the blade to press gently against Dantar's throat.

'All right, enough. I'll just read a book about it,' said Dantar, pushing the sword away.

'Cabin boys don't have books.'

'I'm the son of Calbaras. He has lots of books.'

'Why read books about it if you can't do it?'

'So I can learn how to do it.'

'Have they helped?'

'No,' sighed Dantar.

Suddenly Gyan sniffed the air. 'Not long now,' he said. 'I can smell land.'

Dantar stood up and peered ahead, but he

could not see anything beyond the bank of fog.

'There's only fog ahead,' he said.

'Tomorrow our air and water shapers will disperse the fog,' said Gyan. 'The Savarians will think we appeared out of nowhere, or so the admiral says.'

Gyan did not seem excited by the plan. He sounded tired, even bored.

'Wait a minute, if there's land ahead, it has to be downwind!' exclaimed Dantar. 'How can you smell something downwind?'

'Magic.'

Dantar gave up. Gyan was always friendly, but he talked in riddles. Even though the sun was still above the horizon, it was Dantar's bedtime. His next shift began at midnight, and he needed to be well rested to stay awake on watch. You could get flogged for many things on a warship, but falling asleep on watch got you hanged.

DRAGONS

Three miles above the fleet, the dragon continued to circle. The tiny spark of familiar life was still down there, on the ship he had spared. The spark's essence had even grown a little stronger.

Why do the humans have a dragon chick with them? he wondered again. *Do they know I would spare the ship carrying the infant dragon? Does some puny human dare to shield himself with a young dragon?*

He fought the urge to swoop down, rip the ship apart with his talons and carry the chick away to safety, but knew that humans would treasure it almost as much as himself, so it was not in danger.

Then there was the matter of where it had come from. All dragon eggs were known and accounted for. Study was required, not rescue. Humans had to be watched carefully and closely.

A thousand years ago, the human Dark Hands had grown more powerful than wise, and caused the most terrible war in all of history. The intervention of dragons had wiped out the Dark Hands, and they had woven the master spell to break human magic into four parts.

Perhaps they have forgotten the power of dragons, Dravaud decided. *Perhaps they have forgotten the lesson we taught them, and pretend that it was they who won the victory. We can teach it to them again.*

DANTAR

Being on watch meant pacing the decks while looking out for enemy boarders sneaking over the side to set the ship a-fire. One also had to be alert for officers pretending to be enemy boarders. There were five strokes of the cane for him if he was caught out by an officer. Aside from that, it was easy work. The new admiral had ordered the fleet to furl sails and drop sea anchors. The ships drifted with the current, lit only by Moon and Moonlet.

Moon was high in the sky, casting green light on the fleet. Circling Moon every two hours, Moonlet was said to be a huge dragon guarding Moon. Dantar had believed the story until the day before, when he had seen his first real dragon. *Moonlet is round, and goes through phases, just like Moon*, Dantar decided, looking up at the sky.

Who made up that stupid legend?

A shadow moved, ever so slightly. Dantar seized his alarm whistle with one hand and raised his patrol stick in the other, then spun around. As he expected, another figure was behind him.

'Halt!' he barked. 'Who goes there?'

'Sergeant of irregulars,' came the reply.

'Advance and be recognised.'

By Moon's green light Dantar saw the sergeant's face.

'I wish to report movement by the hatch cover,' said Dantar.

'There's nobody there.'

Around his neck Dantar was wearing a watchman's eye, a phial of seawater full of tiny animals trawled from the sea at the start of his shift. He now drew this out and shook it until the creatures glowed brighter green than Moon's light, lighting up a hooded figure crouching beside the hatch cover. Dantar put the whistle to his lips.

'Stop!' said the sergeant. 'Congratulations, Deckhand Third Class, you passed inspection. Handor, get below.'

How did I know there were two of them? Dantar

wondered once he was alone again. *It was like I felt the sergeant's life force. Did Gyan feel the life force of the people in Savaria, even though they were downwind? Perhaps I have some magic in me after all.*

VELZA

As dawn lightened the sky, Velza took one of the pigeons from the coop under the forecastle and presented it to Gyan. The old wizard englamoured the bird, then released it. A quarter hour later it returned and reported to Gyan in a liquid, warbling language.

'The Savarian coast is close,' he translated. 'Lead me to the captain.'

Velza guided the blind man to the quarterdeck, where he reported what nobody in the entire fleet could see. The admiral was informed, and he gave the order to signal the fleet to haul in the sea anchors and unfurl the sails.

On either side, and as far behind as Velza could see, ships great and small began slicing through the waves, their canvas sails tight from the wind. Until this voyage, she had not realised that there were so many ships in the entire world. She almost felt sorry for the Savarians, but some of the admiral's tactics did not make sense and doubts nagged at her.

'Master Gyan, do the Savarians have oversight birds like your pigeon?' she asked.

'That they do.'

'So they might have sent one to scout behind the fog?'

'Sure to have.'

'So they're ready for us?'

'Aye.'

'Then why did we bother with the fog?'

'Admiral's orders.'

'Why did he order it?'

'He's an idiot.'

'You can't say that, he commands five hundred ships!' Velza exclaimed. So far as she was concerned, the world would be a better place if everyone read rule books, followed orders, and respected people in authority. 'Admirals deserve respect.'

'He's still an idiot.'

'Then why is he in charge?'

'His brother's daughter married the king's grandson.'

So he got his position through family influence! thought Velza. She too had got her position through her father's position, but as a point of honour she went out of her way to prove that she was worthy of the appointment. Most others did not. *Well, with such a large fleet under his command, he can hardly lose*, she decided.

DANTAR

Dantar was taking his mid-shift break and looking for Marko when the oversight pigeon was sent up. Conversations with sailors were generally confined to gambling, wine, girls, fighting, how bad the food tasted, and how much the last flogging hurt, but Marko could talk intelligently about more interesting things. Not only did his friend have shapecasting skills, like Dantar, he could read.

As books had to be copied out by hand they had great value. Marko had told Dantar his father had been a book thief so there were always books in the house. The youth had read dozens of books while they had waited to be sold to new owners. His father had been caught, and his head set upon a pike in the marketplace as a warning to other book thieves. Marko changed his name and found work as a sailor. He was unlucky enough to get caught up in a battle, but lucky enough to do some heroic things while trying to stay alive.

The older boy was on the mid-deck, sitting on a loading hatch-cover and splicing rope damaged by the dragon's attack. There was a large pile of coils of damaged rope beside him. On ships it was always wise to look busy, or someone would put you to work bailing bilge water or scrubbing the decks. Dantar was on a real break, but telling that to an officer would be reported as insolence, and insolence got you punished.

'Need a hand?' said Dantar as he sat down.

'Thanks, but I need more hands than the entire crew has,' Marko replied. 'There's hundreds of bits of damaged rope to splice, and those fixing the rigging are calling for more all the time.'

'Where do I start?'

'Just take any two coils and splice them together, and make it strong but nothing fancy. Everything's sure to get damaged again in the battle that's coming.'

Dantar sat down, trimmed the char away from the rope ends, then began to unravel them.

'You were talking to Gyan yesterday,' said Marko.

'He bet Pandas would only get five strokes,' said Dantar. 'I lost a copper.'

'Pandas might look pathetic, but he does strong fire castings. Once we're on land he'll be worth a hundred marines.'

Yet dragons can do fire castings over water, thought Dantar. *Why can humans only master a single magic – and in my case, no magic at all?*

'I heard that the four human magics used to be one,' Dantar said aloud. 'Do you think that's true?'

Marko nodded. 'Aye. Our magic was split into four parts a thousand years ago. It was too dangerous to have it all together, controlled by a human. Some warlocks could work fire, water, earth and air, all at once. They were called the Dark Hands, because they could reach anywhere. They could even make fire magic work over water.'

'What happened? Nobody can do that today.'

'The kings got all the lesser wizards together to fight the Dark Hands in a magical war. The

Dark Hands lost, and the dragons broke human magic into four parts to stop anyone getting too powerful.'

'But why didn't the Dark Hands win if they were so much better?'

'They were overwhelmed. The warlocks could possess people weaker than themselves, but only one at a time, and only while keeping *focus*. It was like holding down a lever in your head.'

'I've seen heads that were smashed open,' said Dantar. 'There's only grey, squishy stuff inside.'

'That's right, grey, squishy levers,' said Marko, and laughed.

Dantar noticed Velza climbing the steps to the foredeck, followed by Latsar and Pandas. Pandas had his right foot wrapped tightly in sailcloth, and was walking with the aid of a stick.

'Poor sod,' said Dantar. 'I bet it hurts more than his caning.'

'The surgeon charmed the wound,' said Marko. 'He's only feeling a little pain.'

'How do you know that?'

'Velza told me.'

'My snobby sister, the officer? She spoke to you, a common seaman?'

'Lots of important people talk to me. I've been to Savaria and seen their weapons.'

Dantar felt slightly betrayed. Marko was his friend, and friends were meant to have the same enemies. Velza was definitely Dantar's enemy.

'I wish I could do magic,' said Dantar. 'I feel like someone who knows how to cook, but doesn't have any pots and kettles.'

Marko shook his head at the bitterness in Dantar's voice. 'Nothing wrong with being non-magical,' he said. 'I can only raise a strong enough fire casting to light a candle.'

'That's more than I can do.'

'Young Lord Zandale had a ship sunk from under him during the last invasion, but he escaped the Savarians! He did it all without magic.'

'Don't believe that. Anyway, I would have drowned when the ship sank. I can't swim.'

Marko stopped splicing. 'Neither could Zandale.'

'But you said his ship was sunk.'

'Aye, and he held onto a bit of wreckage. Few sailors can swim, but he learned during those ten hours.'

Dantar was not convinced.

'Still wish I could do magic,' he said.

'If you're unlucky, your wish may come true.'

'What's wrong with that?'

'Lord Zandale told me he once wanted to be a hero, and when he reported back about the Deathlight weapon he became a hero. He'd been a common seaman, but the emperor made him a noble and nobles can't be friends with common sailors. The other nobles didn't want to be friends with him because he was too, well, common. Poor Zandale told me he was going to vanish and start a new life as a commoner.'

Dantar cut the charred end off a new length of rope and began unravelling the tarry strands.

'Well then, I wish I had a nicer family.'

'At least you've got a family.'

'My sister despises me, and my mother . . . don't ask. Father's ashamed of me because he's a battle warlock and I'm a nothing. He's only spoken eleven words to me since we sailed.'

'He brought you both on this voyage.'

Dantar's chest tightened. 'Lots of families send their younger sons off to war, hoping they'll die heroically and solve inheritance problems. All four of us cabin boys are from rich families.'

He said the last words in a rush, then looked down. He'd never told anyone about this fear before, and was afraid Marko might laugh. Instead, Marko reached over and punched his shoulder.

'Dantar, do you think the emperor's son sees much of him? Your dad's the most powerful wizard in Dravinia. He's in demand, like the emperor.'

That was true. Battle Warlock Calbaras never had a harsh word for Dantar, but neither did he show warmth. He had heard Velza telling his father that she could only get his attention threatening to set his shoes on fire. At least she *could* set his shoes on fire. All Dantar could do was put them out, using water.

'If the emperor orders your father to be on hand, he can't say no, can he?' Marko continued. 'That'd be treason.'

Treason! Dantar started. The whispers from the speaking tube were treason.

'Something the matter?' Marko asked.

Should I tell him? wondered Dantar. *But what if I misheard? I'd look a fool – and get a flogging – if anyone else found out.*

'Something's worrying you,' Marko insisted. 'I can tell.'

Dantar was starting to shake his head when he heard someone calling orders – and recognised a voice from the speaking tube. He turned, very slowly. Leaning on the foredeck rail, calling out instructions to his water shapers as they practised, was Meslit. He was the best water wizard in the fleet, and the emperor himself had said he was worth a dozen warships.

Something about water wizards unsettled Dantar, they always seemed too thin and pale, as if they had been drowned, then brought back to life. Meslit was one of the tallest aboard, and his robes hung from his limbs and shoulders as if they were soaking wet. Marko said that he had earned his reputation fighting pirates around the islands of the Secaster Archipelago, and that some even thought he had fought with the pirates before being recruited by the emperor.

'You're looking at Meslit,' said Marko.

'Do you smell lamp oil?' asked Dantar, sniffing and turning his head.

'Yes, but don't change the subject.'

'All right, all right. This will sound silly, but

yesterday I was repairing a speaking tube and I heard voices.'

'Sounds logical.'

'Ha ha. They were talking about trusting someone, and a traitor. One of them sounded like Meslit.'

'Meslit?' gasped Marko, suddenly alert and serious. 'Who was the other?'

Dantar shook his head. 'Don't know. Should I tell somebody?'

Marko frowned. 'This is important. We'd better ask someone who can be trusted.'

'Can anyone be trusted?'

'Gyan can.'

Although Dantar now felt like a rabbit emerging from his burrow while a fox was nearby, sharing the secret with someone else was like having a huge weight lifted from his shoulders. The matter was no longer just his responsibility. He coiled up the rope he had been splicing and placed it on the cover of the loading hatch, then set off across the main deck with Marko. They had taken ten paces when a great ball of flames erupted behind them with a blast so loud and intense that Dantar felt the force, rather than really hearing anything.

They were flung through the air and into a group of marines who were drilling nearby.

Dantar pushed himself up from the deck, shaking his spinning head. Through clouds of acrid smoke reeking of lamp oil, he saw that the hatch cover was now a jagged, smoking hole in the deck. His ears were ringing and as he got to his feet the shouting all around him sounded muted.

Marko was sprawled close by, blood trickling from his nose. Dantar staggered over and dropped to one knee. *He's bleeding, that means his heart is working*, thought Dantar. He shook Marko by the shoulders. After a moment Marko opened his eyes, and put a hand to his head.

'What happened?' he asked. 'Dragon?'

'I think someone tried to assassinate us.'

'Only important people get assassinated. We sailors get murdered.'

'But I'm important.'

'Good point.'

VELZA

A crowd of sailors and marines had gathered at the edge of the hole before Velza reached it.

'Make way, officer!' she shouted as she pushed her way past.

Through the smoke, she peered down into the oil store, now a shambles of smashed barrels and broken wood. Pinned under a heavy beam was her father, surrounded by spreading fires. Nearby was a body, dressed in the white tunic of the cook.

'Find a rope!' Velza shouted to the sailor beside her. 'That's an order!'

Rope is not hard to find aboard a sailing ship, and the man was back in moments.

'Tie one end to the mainmast, then take the other to the hole,' she ordered.

Velza tested the knot, then followed the sailor – and saw that Dantar had already climbed down. He was heaving at the beam pinning their father down.

'Find Meslit, tell him there are fires spreading in the hold!' shouted Velza to another sailor.

No other officers were nearby, but she could hear orders being shouted in the distance. This was an oil fire, which at any moment could become an oil explosion. The rule was to fetch the water wizards and stand clear, but the seamen gathered around the hole probably could not read and had not studied the rule books.

Velza looked back into the hold. The fire was licking at her father's boots. In moments his clothing would catch.

Dantar gave up trying to heave the beam off him. 'No good, no good,' he cried to the faces peering down at him.

Velza frantically thought of ways to free her father, or at least save his life. Cut his leg off? Too extreme. Order the sailors down into the blazing hold to lift the beam? They were already frightened, and other officers in the distance were shouting at them to stand clear. Wait for

Meslit to arrive and put out the fire with water magic? That was the only real option.

'Where's Meslit?' she shouted. 'Find Meslit!'

The sailors ignored her. Velza felt very uneasy. Officers who were ignored were often murdered, so that those who ignored them would not be executed for mutiny.

'Pull! Now pull!'

Her brother's voice was faint but distinct. *So that's why I'm being ignored, they think he's in command here.* As the sailors formed into a line to heave on the rope, Velza looked down into the hold again and saw that Dantar had tied the end of the rope to the beam. The sailors heaved and the beam came up a little – just enough for her father to heave himself free.

Dantar cut the rope from the beam and tied it under his father's arms.

'Pull him out! Hurry!' he cried to the sailors.

As soon as her father was safely out, Velza threw the rope back down.

'Dantar, climb the rope!' she cried, but he had collapsed beside the body of Cook.

Flames burn the goodness out of the air, her father had taught her. If that was true, Dantar was suffocating. If she climbed down, she would suffocate too.

'The rope, hold onto the rope!' Velza shouted. 'Dantar! That's an order!'

Orders have an almost magical effect aboard ships – not obeying orders earns a flogging. With his clothes already burning, Dantar lurched into motion, crawled to the rope and grasped. The sailors began to haul him out, and he was almost within reach of Velza's hand when a deluge of water crashed down over him, knocking him back into the oil store.

Velza looked up and saw that Meslit and some of his water shapers had conjured a thick, writhing snake of seawater up over the side of the ship and into the burning hold. Dantar had sunk beneath a mixture of burning oil and seawater.

Now how can someone get himself drowned in the middle of a fire? Velza thought angrily. *That's just typical of my stupid little brother.*

DANTAR

Dantar woke up in dim light, alone. He recognised the cabin to be one of the tiny infirmary rooms because one of his duties was to clean it. The ship was clearly still afloat, which was a relief. However, the walls were definitely at an angle from what Dantar thought should be vertical, meaning that the ship was listing, which was what ships often did before they sank. That was more of a worry, but it was probably because of all the water poured into the hold to put out the fire. A lamp hung from the deck-head and swung to and fro, casting grotesque shadows on the walls.

He groaned and tried to sit up. One of the grotesque looming shadows became Meslit. His eyes were as cold and intense as those of a cat stalking a bird.

He knows, and only Marko could have told him, thought Dantar.

Dantar tried to scramble off the bunk but Meslit was faster. He seized him, pushed him down against the mattress and pressed a hand like steel covered by a silk glove over his mouth. The water wizard leaned closer. The skin of his face was alarmingly white and wrinkled, as if he had spent his entire life submerged. That was the mark of his skill, but it was a seriously disturbing sight.

'I'm sure you agree that a little knowledge is a dangerous thing, boy,' he hissed.

Water gushed out of Meslit's hand and into Dantar's mouth, as if the bilge-pump hose had been jammed between his lips. He struggled, kicking his legs, but Meslit's grip was too strong. Water shot from his nose and flooded down his windpipe.

He was drowning. Again.

Dantar tried to punch Meslit, swinging his arms wildly, hitting at anything he could. His struggles weakened, his vision blurred, and again blackness came for him.

Heat, I can feel heat driving back the water, he

thought, and there were shadows of claws and wings before his eyes as his mind plunged back into blackness.

Dantar heard voices in the blackness.

'How is he?' That was Marko. He sounded worried.

'He'll be all right, I think.'

Dantar opened his eyes to find Marko and the ship's surgeon looking down at him.

'Ah,' said the surgeon. 'You're awake. Always a good sign.'

Marko ruffled Dantar's hair. 'You had us worried,' he said.

Dantar tried to sit up, and gasped in pain. His side felt like it had been punctured by a mass of needles.

'You fell onto some broken timber,' said the surgeon. 'It will hurt for a while, but I've picked the splinters out and applied some oil. What happened in here?'

'What do you mean?'

'The bunk mattress is soaked.'

Not a dream, thought Dantar. *Meslit really did try to drown me, then there was fire everywhere. A fire wizard could do that. Father? There's a small pile of ash on the floor. Did Father save me by burning Meslit? But we're at sea. Fire magic doesn't work at sea.* He recalled shadows of wings and claws. *A dragon? Who would believe that I have a guardian dragon? Not Marko. Best not to mention it.*

'Sorry, can't help,' said Dantar, quite truthfully.

'Well, get up and report for duty,' said the surgeon. 'Others need that bunk.'

'Any word of my father?' asked Dantar. 'Er, that is, Warlock Calbaras?'

'He was well enough to refuse treatment,' said the surgeon. 'Said he had to go into a trance to prepare for the battle, then went to his cabin and locked himself in.'

The surgeon left and Dantar lay back on the wet mattress for a moment, eyeing Marko suspiciously. 'Meslit tried to kill me, and only you could have told him what I overheard,' said Dantar.

'Meslit?' asked Marko. 'Where is he?'

'He, er, had to leave,' said Dantar, who was

very confused about what had happened to Meslit.

'Dantar, you were raving about Meslit before you woke up. That's why I took the surgeon outside, so he wouldn't hear.'

So Meslit might have heard me raving too, but how did he get into the cabin, and out again? wondered Dantar as he got to his feet.

Marko tossed him a sailor's tunic. 'Yours was burned. The owner of that one no longer needs it.'

'What happened? The explosion?'

'Someone lit a fire in the oil store and it blew up. They were probably trying to sink the ship.'

'Who?'

'Well, whoever it was would hardly boast about it, would they? Meslit conjured water out of the ocean to douse the fires. I jumped down, found you unconscious and held your head above the water until help came.'

'My thanks.'

'Any time.'

Dantar stared at the older boy. 'Well, I still think Meslit's a traitor.'

'He saved the ship, nobody will listen to you. Speaking of betrayals, your sister reported that you gave orders to sailors above your rank. That's insolence, which is a flogging offence.'

Dantar sat down on the wet bunk again. He had thought that nothing else could surprise him, but not any more.

'Oh, and by the way, you're a hero.'

Dantar blinked. 'A hero? Me? For what?'

Marko shrugged. 'You saved the fleet's battle warlock. Admiral Dalzico is going to recommend you for a commendation.'

Dantar's eyes went wide. *A commendation*? 'Is that a sort of promotion?' he asked.

'No, it's important people's way of saying thanks without doing very much.'

'I saved the battle warlock just before a battle, yet I get flogged and I don't get a promotion?'

'That's right.'

Above them, men began shouting urgently.

'. . . pump the bilge water out before the fighting starts!'

'I have to go,' said Marko. He stopped at the door. 'The battle's going to be bad, Dantar. Try to stay alive.'

Dantar tried to ignore the pain from his side and back as he struggled into the tunic. Strangely enough, even though his own tunic had been practically burned off his back, there were no burns anywhere on his body.

Looking around the cabin, Dantar noticed that the wall on one side was scorched, except for an unburned, human-shaped patch in the middle. On the floor was damp, greyish ash. *Am I looking at Meslit?* Dantar wondered. *If so, what happened to him?*

VELZA

Again Velza stood before the nine officers of the court of marshal-at-arms in the master cabin. Dressed in his full parade uniform, Marshal Florantas d'Civaros was a daunting figure, even seated at the table. He was from a noble family, but unlike many nobles he was a veteran of thirty years at sea on warships, and was highly respected as a warrior. Beside Velza were Dantar and Calbaras. The warlock explained briefly that he had caught Cook in the act of starting a fire in the oil store. He had tried to wrestle Cook's little lamp away from him, but it was dropped in the struggle and Calbaras only just had time to raise a shield casting before the explosion.

'I was pinned under debris, however,' Calbaras concluded. 'The sailor Dantar climbed down into the wreckage of the store and rescued me.'

'Learned Calbaras, do you have anything to add to Seaman Dantar's account of the rescue?' asked the marshal.

'No, it was quite accurate.'

'In that case, thank you, that will be all. Has anyone been able to find Meslit as yet? No? Very well, we shall move on to Squad Captain Velza's written report on the incident.'

The marshal held up a sheet of reed paper covered in Velza's neat, flowing script.

'You, Squad Captain Velza, are a disgrace to the officers aboard this ship,' he said coldly.

Velza swallowed. She had expected to be commended for getting a rope down into the burning store and sending for Meslit. For a moment she thought he was referring to Dantar, but the marshal had definitely used her name. His attack should have horrified her, but her reaction was instead sheer incomprehension.

'Your brother's a hero, an inspiration that every sailor in the fleet should follow, yet you reported that he gave orders to those of superior rank,' the marshal continued. 'Due to your rank as an officer, your word will stand. The wounded hero of the oil store explosion must receive five strokes of the cane for insolence. *Five lashes*, Captain. And on the eve of battle, when we need the goodwill and loyalty of our sailors and marines. What have you to say for yourself?'

Being forced to defend herself was so totally unexpected that Velza floundered for words. Dantar had ordered the sailors to pull on the rope. Technically, he should have asked her to give the orders. That was what the rules said.

'I, ah, reported exactly what happened,' she said, her words soft and halting.

'The breach was so petty that any other officer would not have mentioned it!' shouted the marshal, slamming his fist down on the table. 'Shapecaster Latsar, step forward. Were there any minor details in your report on Shapecaster Pandas that you could have included but did not?'

After frowning in thought for a moment, Latsar said, 'Yes, Sir.'

'Indeed? Explain.'

'Pandas knows little of weapons. He might

have shot himself without realising the bolt would go right through his foot and pin him to the deck.'

'Why did you not say as much at the inquest?'

'In my judgement, Pandas is not a coward, and I know he would never desert. Why confuse the court with speculation?'

'Squad Captain Velza, what do you say to that?' asked the marshal. 'Shapecaster Latsar exercised judgement. Can you exercise judgement?'

'I – I may have mistaken a plea for help by Dantar as an order. I'm willing to change –'

'You will change nothing!' the marshal shouted. 'We go into battle in a matter of hours, and the sailors and marines must trust their officers absolutely. Officers *never* make a wrong decision or change their minds.'

'Yes, Sir,' said Velza, her voice barely a whisper.

'Deckhand Third Class Dantar, you must be flogged,' said the marshal. 'Five lashes of the cane, it is the law. Please accept my apologies.'

'Sir!' said Dantar smartly.

'Word of this stupidity has spread, and I must repair the damage. Squad Captain Velza, consider yourself unattached and assigned to liaison work on the quarterdeck. Shapecaster Latsar, you are promoted to squad captain and assigned Shapecaster Pandas to command.'

Latsar betrayed me! thought Velza. *That handsome, dashing son of landed gentry betrayed me to get my command! A simple 'No, Sir' would have saved me. I was only being accurate.*

'Deckhand Third Class Dantar, I know you can read,' the marshal was saying. 'Do you know any mathematics?'

'Yes, Sir.'

'Addition, multiplication, vectors?'

'Yes, Sir.'

'Name three navigation instruments.'

'Cross bar, triangulant and logline, Sir.'

'Then you will be the deputy navigator's assistant. It's not much of a rank, but the position outranks a liaisory.'

'Thank you, Sir. Very grateful, Sir.'

'Now then, returning to you, *Liaisory* Velza. After his flogging, Deckhand Third Class Dantar will become a junior attached officer. As an unattached officer, you may not give him orders or discipline him in any way. Violate the code of seniority, and I shall have you before this court again and declared to be . . .' the marshal paused for emphasis, 'a passenger. If your father had not been the fleet's battle warlock you would be dealt with a lot more severely.'

There was more, but Velza's mind had ceased accepting any new words after *passenger*. She was being sent to the quarterdeck as a liaisory. She had followed the rules to the very letter, but her command had been taken away and her brother was to be flogged – then promoted over her. She was not sure which was worse. *What will father say? With luck we may lose the battle and all be killed before I have to explain this over dinner tonight.*

'Is the court in agreement with my decision?' the marshal concluded.

The other officers of the court raised their thumbs. The court rose, and Dantar was taken out to the mid-deck. Here the sergeant of irregulars was waiting with a cane, along with the captain and most of the off-duty men. The sergeant waited for the officers of the court, Calbaras and Velza to take their places.

'Touch your toes, be quick about it, boy,' said the sergeant.

'Please, Sir, I want the cat, not the cane,' said Dantar.

The sergeant blinked. The men stopped joking and making wagers.

'The cane is for those under seventeen,' the sergeant growled. 'You're fourteen. Now bend over and be quick about it!'

'Please, Sir, officers can never be flogged. One day I'll have to command commoners. I want to know what it's like to be flogged before I ever have to order a flogging.'

The sergeant's eyes narrowed. 'It can't be the cat, five lashes would kill you.'

'What about one with the cat and four with the cane – and on my back, like a real sailor?'

The sergeant raised the cane. 'Enough of this nonsense, boy –'

The marshal held up his hand and the sergeant's hand fell to his side. 'Grant his wish, Sergeant. Be quick about it.'

Most of the watching men smiled and nodded.

'Very well,' said the sergeant grudgingly. 'Off with his tunic, tie him to the mast and gag him.'

'I'd rather not be gagged, Sir.'

'It's for you to bite on,' said the marshal. 'Open wide for the sergeant.'

The sergeant delivered four hard, precisely placed strokes with the cane. The single lash with the cat o' nine tails left bleeding cuts on Dantar's back. The entire ship's company cheered as he was untied. Velza was surprised to find herself cheering too, and realised that for the first time she was immensely proud of her younger brother.

'I do believe the boy has done more to restore morale than a double ration of ale,' said the marshal to the sergeant. 'Can he use a sword?'

'More or less.'

'Then put him in charge of five men before the battle and assign that sailor Marko to look after him. Good example to the others.'

'Sir!'

Dantar collapsed on the deck. The cheering drowned his screams when the sergeant poured wine onto his cuts.

'There's dye in the wine, that'll make sure your scars don't fade,' he explained.

'Very grateful, Sir,' gasped Dantar.

'Marshal's orders,' the sergeant said.

Marko, Latsar and Pandas hurried over.

'Come along, Sir, let's get you cleaned up before the battle starts,' said Latsar, as he and Marko helped Dantar to his feet.

The captain strode over to Dantar. He was about half the marshal's age, yet he had the same sort of swagger and authority. He was also the youngest captain in the fleet, and had established his reputation in patrols against the pirates of the Secastar Archipelago. Fifteen years at sea had left him rather too weather-beaten to be called truly handsome, but then good looks were not needed to be a good commander.

'Wear this, it marks you as a navigaton officer,' he explained, handing Dantar a violet crystal on a chain. It was about the length of a finger.

Captain Parvian turned to Velza. 'Come along, Liaisory Velza. New duties.'

Mortified, Velza walked away with him toward the steps of the quarterdeck. All the sailors stood well clear of her, as if she were poisonous.

'Now you understand the fog of battle,' said the captain.

'No, Sir, I don't,' said Velza.

They climbed the steps to the quarterdeck, then Velza followed him past the steersman to the aft rail of the ship. Here the captain folded his arms and gazed out at the fleet that they were leading.

'After any battle, it's easy to find fault with people's actions. Rules can be bent in the fog of battle, and sometimes they *must* be bent. Remember that. Stupid officers are often found dead after battles, and the wounds are always in their backs.'

'Yes, Sir.'

'I've made worse mistakes than yours, but I learned from them. Show what you're made of by learning from this one. The marshal actually admires you in secret.'

'One would never guess it, Sir,' replied Velza, wondering whether the captain was making this up because he was sorry for her.

'It's true, and the other officers call you the Iron Claw. It's probably meant as an insult, but I would be proud of a name like that.'

So, I'm the Iron Claw! thought Velza. *That almost makes up for losing my squad.*

'Your first task will be to find Meslit,' said Parvian. 'Fetch the three remaining cabin boys, have them search the ship and ask everyone when

Meslit was last seen. Going into a naval battle without our most senior water wizard would be very bad for morale.'

Velza now knew that there were unwritten rules for young officer-shapers, and she wanted to learn more of them.

It's so unfair, she fumed to herself. She had obeyed the rules, yet she had lost her squad. *How was I to know rules don't apply to heroes?*

Stationed on the quarterdeck close to Admiral Dalzico and Captain Parvian, Velza saw and heard the preparations for the battle. Dalzico was a huge man with mutton chop whiskers. He towered over Captain Parvian, and the captain was not short. The marshal-at-arms called all the officers together.

'Battle Warlock Calbaras has retired to the master cabin to prepare himself for the attack on the city of Teliz,' the admiral began. 'The fighting will not be long in starting, so all of you should also get in the martial mood, so to speak.'

The admiral was facing aft on the quarterdeck, as if he were addressing the entire fleet. Velza was facing forward with the rest of them, and noticed that there was something wrong with the magically bound fog bank that was moving ahead of the fleet. It seemed less dense than before, in fact she could see a coast and mountains through it.

'The fleet will approach the Savarian capital in a great arc behind the fog,' Dalzico continued, gesturing to the other ships. 'At my signal, two hundred rowboats of marines will set off from the leading ships into the fog. When they land, our air shapers will dissolve the fog and the Savarians will find themselves defeated before they even realise they're being invaded. Any questions?'

Captain Parvian raised his hand.

'What do we do now that the fog has vanished?' he asked.

Dalzico whirled around. The sea was clear all the way to Teliz, Savaria's port city. Judging by the distant alarm bells, the fleet had been noticed.

'The fog's gone!' gasped Dalzico. 'How can that be?'

'Our air shapers created the fog; the Savarian air shapers must have dispersed it,' replied the captain. 'It's also a clear, sunny day, not good for maintaining fog.'

'But it was meant to cover our approach.'

'Quite so, Sir.'

Forty or fifty Savarian galleys were gliding out of the harbour. None were as large as the massive Dravinian warships hurriedly preparing to attack Teliz, but they were fast enough to run down and smash the landing boats.

'They were ready!' Dalzico said. 'They must have been warned.'

It was our emperor who warned them, thought Velza. *You can't gather a fleet of this size without spies noticing. I'm getting really sick of taking orders from stupid people.*

'Orders, Sir?' asked the captain.

'What does our water wizard advise?'

'Meslit has been missing since just after the oil store fire, Sir.'

'Well . . . carry on as before. This doesn't matter, the Savarian defences are puny.'

That's Rule Five from Morale and How to Raise it When Commanding Peasants, thought Velza. *Say something encouraging, even if it's not true. That's a very stupid book.*

'It's important to have some form of battle,' Dalzico said after a moment. 'If the victory is too easy, we will not be honoured as highly.'

That's Rule Three, thought Velza. *If the enemy gains an advantage, tell the men it's part of your plan.*

'The Savarians are positioning their galleys to block our landing boats,' said Parvian. 'They don't expect an attack from our fleet.'

'But that's absurd, of course we shall attack them.'

'I don't like this,' Parvian muttered as he took off his tricorne captain's hat and mopped his brow. 'I've read a report by a survivor of our last invasion attempt. The Savarians have the Deathlight.'

'Deathlight? That weapon is only a sailor's tall tale.'

'If you say so, Sir.'

The admiral snorted and looked down at Parvian, his eyes glaring fiercely as if his flagship's captain were to blame for his plans going awry. Velza wished her father were there to mediate.

'The enemy galleys are small,' said Dalzico. 'With our flamethrowers and ballistas we can obliterate them before they draw close enough to inflict damage.'

'With respect, Admiral, if they are in range, then so are we,' said Parvian.

'Even the dragon disagrees with you!' exclaimed the admiral impatiently, waving at the sky. 'The dragon attacked a ship of *our* fleet – it believes *we* shall be victorious today.'

'Very good, Sir,' said Parvian. 'Do you have any more orders?'

'Attack!'

'Liaisory Velza, have the signaller run up the flags for General Attack.'

Velza saluted, hurried away and passed the order to the signaller, who was stationed beside the stern mast. When she returned, Dalzico's lackey was strapping plate armour onto him. He had been burned by drops of burning pitch after the dragon had attacked, so wearing metal seemed like a sensible precaution.

'And be sure to stuff cloth into the upper joints,' said the admiral. 'I have six burns from being hit by drops of burning pitch yesterday.'

'Regrettable, Sir,' said the lackey.

'My best parade uniform, ruined.'

'Wise not to wear your best into battle, Sir. Except if it's your best armour, of course.'

Velza glanced at the distant city. At the tops of all nine watchtowers there were odd twinklings. The towers were like no buildings she had ever seen; they looked like white stalks, each with a shining, silvery flower at the summit. A lot of work had gone into building them, and she did not believe they were just decorative.

A shout came from the makeshift crow's nest on the mainmast: 'Ship a-fire!'

Parvian spun about and looked up at the crow's nest, then turned in the direction that his lookout was pointing. Nearby, a great battle gallerine was ablaze. The ocean-going galley had a full rig of sails for when the oars were shipped, but those sails were on fire, the entire ship lit by an intense, unnatural light. Velza could see sailors and marines leaping overboard rather than fighting the fires.

'Now it begins,' said Parvian.

The admiral stared at the stricken ship, shielding his eyes from the sun.

'A freak accident, Captain,' said Dalzico. 'Accidents happen.'

'If you say so, Sir,' said Parvian, scanning the rest of the fleet.

'Fire magic doesn't work at sea,' Dalzico continued.

'Another ship a-fire,' called the lookout. 'Off to larboard – and there goes another. And another!'

Bad day for freak accidents, thought Velza.

'What's happening?' demanded Dalzico.

'With respect, Sir, remember the Deathlight weapon that the survivor of the first invasion, Lord Zandale, reported?'

The officers on the quarterdeck were milling about and pointing, aware the *Invincible* was a prime target for whatever was attacking the fleet.

Gallerines, thought Velza. *Our gallerines are being set a-fire first. They're targeting the only ships that can move without wind power. Surely the admiral sees that?*

'They must have spies aboard all our ships, starting fires,' said Dalzico, clearly floundering.

'The fires are in the rigging, out in the open,' said Parvian.

'Then what?' shouted the admiral.

Parvian had spent fifteen years at sea, but Admiral Dalzico was only a nobleman whose family had influence at court. Normally Dalzico had to do no more than point at a city or fleet and shout 'Attack!', then take credit for the victory.

Nine more ships were on fire.

The emperor will not like that, thought Velza. *Ships cost a lot of money.*

'Sails are rubbed with mutton fat to stop them rotting in the damp salt air,' Parvian explained patiently. 'Rigging ropes are coated with tar for the same reason. Start a fire in the sails and rigging, and it's like lighting a candle.' He pointed upwards. 'Everything up there burns easily, Sir.'

'But fire can't work at sea.'

'Fire *magic* can't work at sea, Admiral, but flamethrowers, fire pots and fire arrows don't use magic,' Parvian said. 'The Savarians' Deathlight weapon is some type of flamethrower with a range of miles instead of yards. It's roasting our ships, one by one.'

'Well, do something! Attack the Savarian fleet.'

'We are sailing straight for the Savarian fleet, but the Deathlight weapons are in the city.'

'Fog!' cried the admiral. 'Fog! Have our water and air shapers raise more fog.'

'Waste of time,' said Captain Parvian. 'The enemy shapers can disperse fog as fast as we can raise it.'

'Water shields?'

'Only Meslit can conjure those, and he is still missing.'

'But we can't just sit here and be destroyed!'

'We're attacking, as you ordered.'

'Where is Calbaras? He said our magicians are better than theirs.'

'The Savarians are not using magic! Deathlight is as unmagical as a fire arrow.'

The admiral's mouth opened and closed silently as he searched for words.

He looks like he wants someone to toss him a worm, thought Velza. *Why can't he be charged with being stupid and hanged before he gets anyone else killed?*

'How does Deathlight work without magic?' Dalzico asked at last.

'Mirrors and sunlight,' said Parvian

The admiral's eyebrows rose. 'Mirrors?'

'Yes. Enormous arrays of little mirrors,

polished to perfection. They focus the sun's light into an intense beam. There's one mounted on each of the city's towers.'

'How do you know?'

'It's in the report by a survivor of the first invasion. The Savarians let your fog bank remain complete until it was too late for us to retreat. When we were committed, they unleashed Deathlight.'

The admiral didn't read the report, Velza realised.

'What would you have done?' Dalzico asked.

'Attacked at night. I did recommend a night attack when you first told us your plans. Their weapons are useless without sunlight.'

The admiral's nerve finally broke.

'Do something!' he pleaded. 'Anything!'

'I shall need fleet command, conferred by yourself and witnessed by at least one officer.'

'Yes! Yes! You, Liaisory!' Dalzico strode over to Velza, seized her by the arm and marched her across to the captain. 'Witness that I appoint Captain Parvian as acting admiral!'

He pushed Velza aside. *I might well be murdered if Parvian wins the battle and Dalzico wants to retract his words,* she realised. *I'm pretty sure the rule book doesn't say it's my duty to be murdered so that a nobleman doesn't look stupid.*

'Liaisory, go to the signaller,' said Parvian. 'Raise flags for *sweeps* and *fire alert*.'

The captain had ordered all sails to be furled, right across the fleet. The decks were to be doused with water, and more water was to be kept ready. Each ship had a few long sweep-oars for docking, and these would now be used. They were not as effective as sails, but they worked.

Even with the sails furled ships caught fire, but more slowly than before. The tarry ropes burned like candle wicks, and rained burning tar down onto the decks and furled sails. Huge plumes of smoke like thunderclouds twisted into the sky.

'We're doomed,' Dalzico croaked, taking his polished helmet off and flinging it to the deck.

'Not at all,' explained Parvian. 'The smoke from our burning ships is blowing ahead of the fleet, protecting us from the mirror weapons. Ships in the vanguard are being set on fire, but those behind will move closer to the city before they burn. When we are near, we shall be attacked by the Savarians' galleys. However, a few landing boats will get through.'

'But – but we may well lose three quarters of the fleet.'

'Maybe more. It will not be an easy, glorious victory.'

'How will I explain the losses at court?'

'I can't say, Admiral, I'm not a courtier. Come with me to the mid-deck.'

'But we command from the quarterdeck.'

'The quarterdeck is exposed to the mirror weapon.' Parvian shouted for all to hear, 'All officers, down to the mid-deck. Steersman, get below, steer from the storm cabin. I'll call directions through the speaker tubes.'

For a moment Velza saw the admiral's eyes, and they were wide with fear. *Does a rabbit look like that when cornered by a fox?* she wondered. *If the enemy does not kill him, the emperor will. Everyone with any sense fears death, but is Dalzico also desperate to stay alive? If he is, what might he do?*

▽△△▽

During her training Velza had been told that it was never easy to follow a battle from within the battle, especially with smoke everywhere. Nobody is really sure where to go, whom to shoot at, or who is winning. At first Velza had a very good view of the battle, and she wondered whether the old veteran who taught at the Imperial Marine Academy knew what he was talking about.

The Savarians had set all five Dravinian gallerines alight, and that made the situation much simpler. If a ship had one mast and dozens of oars, it was Savarian. If it had three masts and six oars, it was Dravinian. Deathlight could not penetrate the smoke, but the Savarian galleys could – and they had bow rams.

Velza stayed close to the captain and admiral, ready to do as ordered. Suddenly Captain Parvian seemed to remember her.

'You, Liaisory Velza, can you use a sword?' he called.

'I have a fencing certificate from –'

'Then stay on the mid-deck and defend the admiral if we're boarded.'

'But Sir, surely I should call his personal guard.'

'The real admiral had a personal guard, but he and his guards died when the *Intrepid* was destroyed yesterday. Dalzico was so confident about victory that he did not bother to appoint a personal guard squad, and his lackey is just a barber and tailor.'

I've just been made the admiral's personal guard, thought Velza, *but nobody will know unless it goes into a report and it won't. It's not fair, reports should be fair!* Through swirls of smoke Velza saw that one of the small, fast Savarian galleys was heading straight for the flagship. Unless it was stopped, its ram would go through the larger vessel's hull. Ballistas shot firepots of oil at the galley, and plumes of fire burst on its long, flat deck. As burning oil leaked down onto the rowers, the oars lost rhythm and the galley slowed.

Captain Parvian hurried over to a speaking tube bolted to the mainmast and pulled a large cork on a chain out of the mouthpiece funnel.

'Steersman, turn twenty degrees to port!' he shouted.

The flagship began to turn, and the angle between the two ships lessened. The galley needed to hit the side squarely for its ram to pierce the hull, but on this angle it could only achieve a glancing blow. Velza winced at the sound of a drawn out, splintering crash as the flagship collided with the galley, smashing away the oars along one side.

Dalzico looked frantic with terror. 'We're sinking!' he shouted. 'Launch the gigboats!'

'Their ram did not strike hard enough to hole us,' called the captain.

The flagship emerged from the smoke into clear air, and Velza saw that Teliz was close.

'Their air shapers are clearing the smoke away so Deathlight can burn us,' said Parvian. 'Where's Calbaras? He should be leading our shapecasters; our air shapers should be fighting back.'

'Another galley attacking!' shouted the man in the crow's nest.

Suddenly the light around the *Invincible* became so bright that it seemed like the sun had dropped on them. Those on the mid-deck were shadowed by the forecastle, but the crews of the arbalests and ballistas on the forecastle and quarterdeck were directly exposed to the blast of light and heat from one of the Deathlight towers. Some men leapt overboard, others roasted where they stood. The lookout left the crow's nest and ran along a yardarm with his clothes and hair on fire, then jumped into the water, leaving a trail of smoke as he fell.

'Steersman, return twenty degrees to starboard,' shouted the captain into the speaking tube.

Drops of burning tar rained down onto the deck from the masts and rigging, which were ablaze. On the shadowed mid-deck everyone held cloaks and jackets over their heads, and sailors and marines ran about carrying buckets of water to douse the flames. Paint blistered, and even the timbers and planks smoked and charred.

The Savarian galley was much closer, and Velza realised what the enemy was doing. Deathlight was making the flagship defenceless while the galley approached, and as soon as the galley rammed them it would be focused on another ship.

Marines and sailors crouched with their crossbows ready, waiting for targets on the Savarian ship to come within range. The ship's air and water shapers were gathered near the steps to the foredeck, chanting hoarsely as they tried to raise the fog. The enemy shapecasters were keeping the air clear from the shore, and raising breezes to blow the smoke aside.

Why is father not helping? Velza wondered. *He went below to prepare for the battle, but surely he must be ready by now.* Only the admiral could command him, but the captain was now the admiral and he was busy trying to defend the ship and save the fleet. *Father might listen to one of his children,* Velza thought. She could not leave the mid-deck because she had been ordered to protect Dalzico, but Dantar was another matter.

Velza struggled with her conscience. Her conscience lost.

Sometimes you have to be bad for the greater good, she decided, running across to where Dantar was standing with Marko and five marines. She saluted.

'Orders from the admiral, go to Calbaras in the master cabin,' she said, pointing aft. 'Tell him he's needed on deck.'

'You can't give me orders,' Dantar began.

'It's the admiral's orders, she's only passing them on,' said Marko, picking up the dousing pail. 'Wrap your hands in the dousing cloths, and hold still.'

Dantar handed his crossbow to a marine, then Marko emptied the pail of water over him as he wrapped the cloths around his hands.

'Marko, Velza, er, goodbye, probably,' said Dantar, and he hurried off.

'Why did you do that to a superior officer?' demanded Velza.

'The door leading to the master cabin is directly exposed to the heat from Deathlight,' Marko replied. 'Being wet may protect him a little.'

Velza realised that the door under the quarterdeck was blackened and smoking from the Deathlight's heat. She screamed at Dantar to stop, but it was too late.

DANTAR

For Dantar, it was a choice between getting hanged for disobeying an order and being roasted alive. *I'm dead either way, so I'd better die for a good reason*, he decided. *Dead at fourteen, what a joke. I'll never grow a beard, meet girls or drink wine.*

He kept to the forecastle's shadow as long as he could, crouching low. Staying within the thinner shadow of the mainmast, he moved closer. The door leading to the master cabin was across ten feet of exposed decking – smoking under Deathlight's merciless heat.

'This will really hurt!' Dantar said to himself as he prepared for the dash to the door – then he realised that his voice had broken and was much deeper. 'Oh great, I get to die with a grown-up voice,' he muttered as he ran.

By the time Dantar reached the door his

clothes were smoking and beginning to crumble, yet his hair was not alight and his skin was not even blistering. The wet douse cloths around his hands hissed as they touched the hot metal of the latch, but it clacked open easily. He slipped inside the storm cabin, a sheltered space from where the steersman could steer the ship in bad weather, guided by orders through the speaking tube. Dantar slammed the door shut.

The douse cloths fell from his hands, burned to crumbling char. Nothing made sense. The beam from Deathlight had been uncomfortably warm, but not furnace hot.

'How goes the battle?' the steersman asked, one hand on the huge tiller lever and the other holding a speaking tube to his ear. 'They only tell me where to steer.'

'It's bad, but the smoke's shielding us from the heat weapon,' Dantar lied, trying to be optimistic. 'Where's Calbaras?'

'In the master cabin, through the door behind me. Why doesn't he help us fight?'

'I was sent here to find out.'

Dantar went to the door.

'Mind the handle, it glows hot if you touch it!'

warned the steersman, but Dantar had already grasped it.

The handle was red hot in his hand, but to him it was merely warm. *Sweat*, he thought as he pulled the door open. *The sweat on my skin must be protecting me from hot things.*

Calbaras was seated in the captain's carved wooden chair, his hands resting on the padded arms. The court's table had been pushed to one side.

'Father?'

Calbaras did not answer.

Dantar edged closer. The warlock's eyes were unfocused.

Working some kind of spell, Dantar thought. Although he did not know how to cast spells, he knew better than to interrupt. That would be dangerous for both of them.

As he waited, more charred cloth fell from the sleeve of his tunic. The fabric was blackened and crumbling from Deathlight's heat, yet his skin was still not blistered or red. He could hear the sounds of the battle from outside, and the windows showed burning ships and billowing smoke.

It can't be just sweat or water protecting me, he thought. *It has to be magic. Fire magic that works over water. Only dragons can do that, but dragons are bigger than this ship. Or are they? How big are young dragons? Maybe a dragon chick is following me around, shapeshifted into a seagull. Why would it be protecting me? Maybe dragons like totally unmagical humans.*

His father had a strange, powerful aura, and he was the same age and build as the marshal, with broad shoulders, greying hair and eyebrows like deck brushes. If they ever had a fist fight, you could never pick who would win. Dantar circled his father once, then stood before him, hoping that he would notice him in spite of the trance. It was like standing in front of a loaded arbalest.

Although his father took Dantar everywhere, he hardly had anything to do with him. Apart from the fire in the oil store, this was the first time Dantar had been alone with him for the entire voyage. Calbaras blinked. Dantar flinched back. Slowly, carefully, as if emerging from a deep sleep, Calbaras stood up and glared down at Dantar.

'Boy, what is it?' he demanded. 'Why are you here?'

'Admiral's orders. The battle's going badly, he

wants you outside, commanding our wizards and shapers.'

'I see everything, and I see our fleet winning. Tell that to the admiral.'

That did not sound right to Dantar. The admiral's attack had become a fiasco.

'Wait, please, there's something else,' Dantar pleaded. 'I heard people talking on a speaking tube I was repairing. They were planning to betray the ship. One of them was Meslit, the water wizard. He tried to drown me, twice.'

Calbaras's eyes widened with surprise and interest.

'Have you told anyone else?' he asked, grasping Dantar by the arms.

Oh great, so father finally hugs me, just as we're about to die.

'I've only told Marko, he's my friend, a sailor.'

'You should have come to me first.'

'You're always busy, father.'

'I'm never too busy to flush out treason.'

'Is it too late?' asked Dantar, who felt very stupid.

'No, I can still save the day.'

Calbaras lifted Dantar from the floor and flung

him straight through the leadlight window in the side of the cabin.

Dantar burst through the glass and lead strips. He thought that the worst was over, and that hitting the water would be like jumping onto a pile of feather cushions. A moment later he smacked into the water, and it felt as hard as the *Invincible*'s deck, knocking the wind out of him. When he tried to gasp for air, there was only water, and it was no more breathable than the water he had nearly drowned in earlier that day.

I can't breathe water and I can't swim, he thought. *My own father threw me overboard. How much worse can it get?*

VELZA

On deck, the glare from the heat weapon suddenly ceased.

'They gave up!' shouted Admiral Dalzico, almost hysterical with relief. 'We beat them!'

'They turned the beam away because they don't want to burn their own people,' Parvian replied.

'What? You mean there are Savarian spies aboard?'

'No, but there'll soon be dozens of Savarian marines. They will hit us square-on this time, and we will be boarded and sunk.'

The captain pointed to a Savarian war galley being rowed straight for them. The galley had not been hit by a barrage of firepots, and was closing in at ramming speed and under full control.

Dalzico was suddenly faced with hand-to-hand

fighting. The prospect of this sliced through the last of his control.

'I surrender, we all surrender!' he shouted. 'Wave the surrender flag!'

He thinks the enemy will spare him and demand a huge ransom, thought Velza. *He would rather trade the entire fleet for his life. Beware of those who value their lives too highly.*

'Liaisory, fetch a white cloth!' cried Parvian. 'Admiral, hurry, come to the rail so the enemy can see you waving.'

Where can I find something white in the middle of a battle? Velza wondered as she watched the captain and admiral running to the edge of the deck. Captain Parvian had a hand on Dalzico's back, pushing him along. The admiral was wearing a hundred pounds of metal armour, so that as he reached the rail he had too much momentum to stop. He crashed into it, toppled over and fell to the waves below.

The captain just murdered the admiral! Velza realised as she hurried over. She looked around. The officers and men nearby were smiling.

'Our story is that the admiral ran to the railing,

overbalanced and fell into the sea,' Parvian said calmly.

'But, Sir –'

'Or I'll make sure you hang alongside me.'

'Yes, Sir. Fog of battle, Sir.'

'That's the attitude, Liaisory Velza. Now take off your cloak and surcoat."

'Yes, Sir, but why?'

'Because you can swim better without them.'

As Parvian walked away, Velza bundled up her cloak and surcoat, then flung them over the side. There was no sign of the admiral. Dressed in steel plate armour, he had sunk like a stone and would be dead already. Suddenly a small body burst through the side window of the master cabin and splashed into the water.

That's Dantar! thought Velza.

Without another thought, Velza vaulted the railing and plunged into the water, then struck out for where Dantar had sunk. Moments later, the bow ram of the Savarian galley smashed into the side of the *Invincible*.

DANTAR

Dantar was drowning for the third time that day. *You always take breathing for granted until you can't do it any more*, he thought amid the terror of trying to breathe water.

When he saw the girl swimming towards him, he thought that he had died already and that she was a blessed spirit come to take him to the afterlife. She was beautiful, pale and graceful, and suddenly Dantar realised that he was to be taken up to the clouds of the blessed, and not the fires of underground torment. *She's Celmorae, the Ferrygirl, come to take me to paradise.*

The illusion shattered as the girl seized him by the hair and began swimming upwards. His head broke the surface, and for a few moments nothing was more important than gulping air. The beautiful, pale girl had become his angry, dishevelled older sister. To his astonishment, she saluted, then pushed a piece of wreckage at him.

'Respectfully request that you grab this piece of driftwood and don't drown, Sir!' barked Velza.

'You – you jumped overboard to rescue me!' Dantar spluttered. 'You deserted.'

'Yes, Sir, and if anyone's left alive, they'll hang me. Now pardon me while I swim ashore and continue to desert – Sir!'

My sister cares about me! thought Dantar as he stared after her, then glanced back at the *Invincible*. She was sinking – and dragging the Savarian galley down with her. Returning to his post was not an option.

Dantar began kicking his legs, steering his piece of driftwood in the direction of the shore. In spite of all the horrors and danger that surrounded him, Dantar felt strangely happy. *Velza saved me!* For the very first time, he felt part of a loving family.

DRAGONS

High above the battle, the dragon grew alarmed. The dragon chick was frightened. Its faint, distant aura was becoming cold. Alarm became anger, and anger became fury.

How dare they endanger a dragon chick with their petty battles? I shall pluck the chick from danger, annihilate both fleets and burn the city.

Wings that could shadow a castle folded back, and Dravaud dropped like a shooting star toward the battle. A power greater than all the warships in the entire world had been unleashed, and nothing could call it back.

TO BE CONTINUED in *Dragonfall Mountain*

More great reading from Ford Street Publishing

THE WARLOCK'S CHILD
BOOK TWO
Dragonfall Mountain

The *Invincible* has been attacked, and all seems lost. Dantar's only escape from his enemies is through the foul-smelling sewers of Savaria.

Velza's plans to save him are soon thwarted by three enormous dragons threatening to set fire to the city.

Can Dantar and Velza deliver the city from danger?

When two of Australia's most popular fantasy authors collaborate, *The Warlock's Child* weaves a new and exciting brand of magic.

RRP $12.95
Release May 2015

PAUL COLLINS & SEAN McMULLEN

www.fordstreetpublishing.com   FORD ST

More great reading from Ford Street Publishing

THE WARLOCK'S CHILD

READ ALL SIX BOOKS

THE BURNING SEA	April
DRAGONFALL MOUNTAIN	May
THE IRON CLAW	June
TRIAL BY DRAGONS	July
VOYAGE TO MORTICAS	August
THE GUARDIANS	September

When two of Australia's most popular fantasy authors collaborate, *The Warlock's Child* weaves a new and exciting brand of magic.

RRP $12.95

PAUL COLLINS & SEAN McMULLEN

www.fordstreetpublishing.com   FORD ST

More great reading from Ford Street Publishing

BOOK 1 IN THE JELINDEL CHRONICLES

PAUL COLLINS

Dragonlinks

An all-powerful, enchanted mailshirt from the stars.
Six links are missing.
An orphan, a streetwise urchin and a swordsman must find the links before the greatest evil known descends upon Q'zar.

'Dragonlinks offers compulsive reading in a thrilling and wonderfully imagined quest for the individually power-bestowing links of a mysterious and arcane mailshirt. The story performs the unusual feat of combining meticulous and original world-building with a matchless heroine in the extraordinary young Countess Jelindel.'
ISOBELLE CARMODY

www.fordstreetpublishing.com

FORD ST

More great reading from Ford Street Publishing

BOOK 4 IN THE JELINDEL CHRONICLES
PAUL COLLINS
Wardragon

A sorceress, A swordsman, A thieving larrikin
...and their deadliest foe, the omnipotent Wardragon

'Wardragon is the culmination of The Jelindel Chronicles in a soaring saga. Finally Jelindel, with her allies Zimak and Daretor, has tracked the alien mailshirt across two radically different worlds.

'But the journey is perilous when each step is lined with flying beasts, metal wasps, mercenaries and assassins ... and the mailshirt linked up with the evil Preceptor to create a deadly enemy.

'All Jelindel has is a little magic, Zimak's wit and Daretor's sword to scrape through and that is not enough.'
ALLAN BAILLIE

'Collins captures a terrifying, tense world with a touch of humour and holds it to the last shattering battle.' ALLAN BAILLIE

www.fordstreetpublishing.com   FORD ST

More great reading from Ford Street Publishing

QUENTARIS
QUEST OF THE LOST CITY

The Spell of Undoing
by Paul Collins

Calamity has befallen the city of Quentaris!

Due to a vengeful plot by warlike Tolrush, Quentaris is uprooted — city, cliff-face, harbour and all — and hurled into the uncharted rift-maze. Lost and adrift in this endless labyrinth of parallel universes, encountering both friend and foe, the city faces a daunting task. Somehow, Quentaris must forge a new identity and find its way home.

And nothing is ever as easy as it seems ...

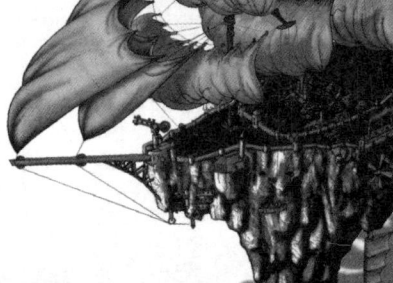

www.fordstreetpublishing.com

FORD ST